HELLO, I'm THEA!

I'm Ge[...]

As I'm sure y[...] [...]

bestselling novels, I'm a special co[...]

for *The Rodent's Gazette*, Mouse Island's most famous newspaper. Unlike my 'fraidy mouse brother, I absolutely adore traveling, having adventures, and meeting rodents from all around the world!

The adventure I want to tell you about begins at Mouseford Academy, the school I went to when I was a young mouseling. I had such a great experience there as a student that I came back to teach a journalism class.

When I returned as a grown mouse, I met five really special students: Colette, Nicky, Pamela, Paulina, and Violet. You could hardly imagine five more different mouselings, but they became great friends right away. And they liked me so much that they decided to name their group after me: the Thea Sisters! I was so touched by that, I decided to write about their adventures. So turn the page to read a fabumouse adventure about the

THEA SISTERS!

Colette

She has a passion for clothing and style, especially anything pink. When she grows up, she wants to be a fashion editor.

Paulina

Cheerful and kind, she loves traveling and meeting rodents from all over the world. She has a magic touch when it comes to technology.

Violet

She's the bookworm of the group, and she loves learning. She enjoys classical music and dreams of becoming a famouse violinist.

THE THEA SISTERS

WITHDRAWN

Nicky

She comes from Australia and is very enthusiastic about sports and nature. She loves being outside and is always ready to get up and go!

Pamela

She is a great mechanic: Give her a screwdriver and she'll fix anything! She loves pizza, which she eats every day, and she loves to cook.

Do you want to help the Thea Sisters in this new adventure? It's not hard — just follow the clues!

When you see this magnifying glass, pay attention: It means there's an important clue on the page. Each time one appears, we'll review the clues so we don't miss anything.

**ARE YOU READY?
A NEW MYSTERY AWAITS!**

AND THE
RAINFOREST
RESCUE

Scholastic Inc.

Copyright © 2019 MONDADORI LIBRI S.p.A. per Edizioni Piemme Italia. International Rights © Atlantyca S.p.A. English translation © 2020 by Atlantyca S.p.A.

The publisher does not have any control over and does not assume any responsibility for author or third-party websites or their content.

GERONIMO STILTON and THEA STILTON names, characters, and related indicia are copyright, trademark, and exclusive license of Atlantyca S.p.A. All rights reserved. The moral right of the author has been asserted. Based on an original idea by Elisabetta Dami. geronimostilton.com.

Published by Scholastic Inc., *Publishers since 1920,* 557 Broadway, New York, NY 10012. SCHOLASTIC and associated logos are trademarks and/or registered trademarks of Scholastic Inc.

Stilton is the name of a famous English cheese. It is a registered trademark of the Stilton Cheese Makers' Association.

No part of this publication may be reproduced, stored in a retrieval system, or transmitted in any form or by any means, electronic, mechanical, photocopying, recording, or otherwise, without written permission of the copyright holder. For information regarding permission, please contact: Atlantyca S.p.A., Via Leopardi 8, 20123 Milan, Italy; e-mail foreignrights@atlantyca.it, atlantyca.com.

This book is a work of fiction. Names, characters, places, and incidents are either the product of the author's imagination or are used fictitiously, and any resemblance to actual persons, living or dead, business establishments, events, or locales is entirely coincidental.

ISBN 978-1-338-65513-1

Text by Thea Stilton
Original title *Destinazione Malesia*
Art director: Iacopo Bruno
Cover by Barbara Pellizzari, Giuseppe Facciotto, and Flavio Ferron
Illustrations by Barbara Pellizzari Vleria Barmbilla, Chiara Belleello, Federico Giretti, Antonia Campo, and Flavio Ferron
Graphics by Alice Iuri / theWorldofDOT

Special thanks to Becky Herrick
Translated by Lidia Tramontozzi
Interior design by Becky James

10 9 8 7 6 5 4 3 2 1   20 21 22 23 24

Printed in the U.S.A.   40
First printing 2020

ARE WE EVEN GOING?

A **wind** blew away the clouds that had covered Whale Island in a light blanket of **snow** that morning. A little sparrow left its perch on a branch and **flew** toward a window on the second floor of Mouseford Academy.

From inside her room, Paulina saw the little bird pecking at the **seeds** she'd placed out on the window ledge. She smiled, then turned back to her room, where the **THEA SISTERS** had gathered to spend the cold winter afternoon.

"Sisters, when we leave for

our **Malaysian adventure**," Colette was squeaking, "I **promise** to take only a backpack! Mouse's honor!"

Nicky looked down at the mug of tea she was holding between her paws and muttered, "We still don't know **if we will actually be able to go** . . ."

Paulina **SQUEEZED** her roommate's paw. "I know you've dreamed about taking this

exciting trip for a long time," she squeaked. "I'm sure that before long, we'll all be packing our **BAGS** with smiles on our snouts!"

The invitation to go to Malaysia had come a few weeks earlier from two Malaysian friends of the Thea Sisters, **Latifah** and **Ramlee**. They were famouse on the Internet for their blog, **Two Friends and a Suitcase**, where they wrote about their travels around the world.

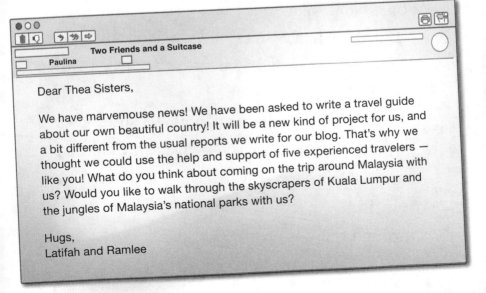

Two Friends and a Suitcase

Paulina

Dear Thea Sisters,

We have marvemouse news! We have been asked to write a travel guide about our own beautiful country! It will be a new kind of project for us, and a bit different from the usual reports we write for our blog. That's why we thought we could use the help and support of five experienced travelers — like you! What do you think about coming on the trip around Malaysia with us? Would you like to walk through the skyscrapers of Kuala Lumpur and the jungles of Malaysia's national parks with us?

Hugs,
Latifah and Ramlee

The Thea Sisters had emailed back as **FAST** as the mouse ran up the clock.

See you soon!

They'd never been to Malaysia, and they could go during their **Vacation**! On their last video call, their blogger friends said: "Focus on your exams for now. When you're all done, we'll send you **TRAVEL** details!"

But the Thea Sisters had finished all their exams and still hadn't heard a squeak from **Latifah** and **Ramlee**.

"Sisters, I have an idea!" Pamela squeaked, trying to get the mouselets back into a good mood. "While we wait to hear from our **friends**, we could still take a little walk through the **JUNGLE**!"

Look!

She held up a **FLYER** from the Whale Island movie theater.

"*MY LIFE IN THE JUNGLE*," Violet read aloud from the flyer. "What's that?"

Pam smiled. "It's about an explorer who spends ten years in the rainforest studying the **animals** that live there. How about it? It might be a fun way to get in the jungle mood!"

They all loved Pam's idea. Soon, the Thea Sisters sat in the **DARKNESS** of the movie theater, watching the film. Halfway through, while the explorer on the SCREEN was watching a group of flying squirrels, Paulina felt her bag vibrate.

Oops! I think I forgot to turn off my MousePhone for the movie! she thought. *Good thing the sound is off!*

Paulina turned her attention back to the film but was distracted by a thought: Did her phone vibrate because an important **email** arrived? Normally, she would never check her phone while at the movies, but today, she was as curious as a cat.

Oops! I forgot to turn off my phone!

She quietly pulled out her **phone** and looked at the screen. Latifah and Ramlee had sent her an email! Paulina opened it and broke into a big smile.

"Mouselets, take a look!" she whispered, passing the phone to her friends. They each read the email, eyes SHINING with happiness.

The friends didn't need to discuss it — they all got up and silently scurried out of the theater.

"What happened?" asked the mouse at the

Two Friends and a Suitcase

Paulina

Hi, Thea Sisters!

We're sorry for the long silence, but we've been so busy preparing for the trip! The plane tickets to Kuala Lumpur are attached here. Are your bags packed???

We can't wait to see you!
Latifah and Ramlee

ticket booth when he saw them *hurrying* through the exit. "Didn't you like the movie?"

"Oh, it was **fabumouse**!" Paulina said, smiling. "We'll finish seeing it another time. Right now, a real **JUNGLE** adventure is waiting for us!"

WELCOME TO KUALA LUMPUR!

Latifah and **Ramlee** had thought of everything! Not only did they plan the entire expedition across **West Malaysia**, the area they would be writing about, but they also booked everything the Thea Sisters would need!

Just a few days later, the five mouselets were walking off a plane in **Kuala Lumpur**, the capital of Malaysia.

"Latifah and Ramlee are worth their weight in **cheese**," squeaked Colette. "We are so lucky. I can't believe they invited us on this amazing trip!"

Nicky nodded. "After reading their **BLOG**, writing so many emails, and seeing each

MALAYSIA

Malaysia is located in **Southeast Asia**. It is made up of two separate regions: West Malaysia and East Malaysia. West Malaysia is also called **Peninsular Malaysia**, since it is on the Malay Peninsula. It shares borders with Thailand on the north and Singapore on the south. East Malaysia is on the island of **Borneo**. It borders Indonesia on the south, and it surrounds the little country of Brunei.

When traveling through Malaysia, tourists can go from the **futuristic architecture** of cities like Kuala Lumpur to the **wild vegetation** of the rainforest very quickly. Travelers can dip themselves into the **diverse** environment that results from the customs and traditions of the many different cultures that make up the population. These include Malay, Chinese, Indian, and other South Asian cultures.

Continent: Asia

Capital: **Kuala Lumpur**

Official Language: **Malay**

Currency: **Ringgit**

other on video calls, it actually feels as if we've already TRAVELED with them."

"Now we're finally having this adventure together!" Violet finished for her.

As they left the airport terminal, sliding doors opened and revealed Latifah and Ramlee. They held up a sign that said THEA SISTERS and looked as happy as mice at an all-you-can-eat cheese buffet.

"You have no idea how excited we are to be here!" Nicky called to them. "We love your blog, and now we get to be a part of it!"

Pam nodded. "The way you describe your travels is so inspiring, Latifah!"

"And so are your photos, Ramlee!" added Paulina.

"And together they really take readers with you on your adventures!" Colette said, meshing her paws together.

Latifah smiled a big smile. "We need to thank you, too! Since we started taking your advice, our blog has gotten so much better. Not to mention, far more popular!"

"Are you ready to travel with us through **Malaysia**?" asked Ramlee with a big grin.

The Thea Sisters looked at one another, and all squeaked, "**YESSSS!**"

As they loaded their luggage into a van, Latifah rattled off the **itinerary** she'd planned.

"We won't waste a single moment. Tomorrow we'll explore the *natural wonders* of the Malay Peninsula. Today, we'll tour Kuala Lumpur."

"The first chapters of our travel guide will

Today we visit the city!

Fabumouse!

focus on the capital city," Ramlee said.

"Great!" exclaimed Nicky. "What will our first stop be?"

"That's a surprise!" Latifah smiled as she revved the engine. "But I can tell you that it's a very special place!"

They drove toward the city and soon came to a white building topped by large domes and SPINDLY TOWERS.

"This is Kuala Lumpur's old TRAIN STATION," explained Ramlee. "Today, few trains pass through it, but it was once the main railway hub in the city."

"You're right: This *is* a very special place," agreed Violet. She was **fascinated** by the unique architecture of the building.

Latifah grinned. "It's special not only because it's considered to be one of the most beautiful stations in the world but also

because it's the place where my *friendship* with Ramlee began!"

The mouselet described the sunny afternoon a few years earlier when she and Ramlee had met by chance in front of the building. They just started chatting and found they shared the same passion for traveling.

"And a couple of weeks later, we decided to see more of the world together and start our own BLOG!"

"What a great story," Colette said. "Think of it: If this building weren't here, you NEVER would have met! Then your blog wouldn't exist, so we would never have read it, so we wouldn't be friends, and we wouldn't be here, and — crusty cheddar! That's enough! I don't like where that's going!"

They all burst out laughing, except for

Paulina. She leaned in and whispered, "Look at that **strange rat** over there — he's been staring at us . . ."

"Oh! That's Safiq," Ramlee said. "He'll be our guide. We told him to meet us here so we could **introduce** him to you," he explained.

He motioned Safiq over and said to him, "These are our friends, who —"

Safiq's cell phone rang, interrupting the introduction. He answered it and walked away without a squeak to the other mice.

"I guess he's not a big talker . . ." joked Pam, as Safiq continued his phone call.

Ramlee smiled. "You're right. He's

rather quiet, but he knows the parks we'll be visiting like the back of his **PAW**. He's highly recommended."

"Actually, Safiq had told us that he was too **busy** to guide us," Latifah told the Thea Sisters. "Then, a couple of days ago, he called to say he was **FREE**."

I'm free!

Safiq returned to the group . . . but only briefly. When he heard that they were about to begin **touring** the city, he shook his snout with a scowl.

"I can't join you, but I'll see all of you tomorrow. And **DON'T BE LATE**!

Great!

We don't want to be waiting around for any mouse," he warned.

"Oh well," Latifah said as Safiq walked away. "We'll have plenty of time to get to know him when he takes us through the **WILD JUNGLE**. Today, Ramlee and I will take you through the **URBAN JUNGLE**!"

FABUMOUSE FASHION

The Thea Sisters were expert travelers. They were used to gathering **information** on the places they visited and planning out **interesting** stops well before their trip began. This time, however, they didn't need to, because they had two guides who couldn't wait to take them sightseeing in the mousetastic **Malaysian** capital!

"We're going to places we think everyone

KUALA LUMPUR

Kuala Lumpur is the **capital of Malaysia** and the largest city. It's a thriving metropolis full of both **modern and traditional architecture** as well as large **natural spaces**. In the Malaysian language, *Kuala Lumpur* means **"muddy estuary."** The name was chosen because the city, which originated in 1857, stands where the Klang and Gombak Rivers combine.

passing through **Kuala Lumpur** should visit," explained Ramlee. "And if you like them, it will confirm that they are **interesting** spots and deserve a place in our guide!"

As they chatted, the group arrived in front of a **low building** with a light blue facade.

"Central Market," read Colette. "That sounds like a shopping center to me. **Fabumouse!**" Colette had a passion for fashion and loved to shop.

The friends entered the market and strolled by its **UNiQUE** shops. **Soft music** played in the background.

"As you read at the entrance, the Central Market of **Kuala Lumpur** has been here since 1888," Latifah said.

"Initially it was a food market, and later it became a **craft market**," added Ramlee.

"There are sections devoted to each of the **THREE** main cultures in our country: Malaysian, Chinese, and Indian!"

The Thea Sisters wandered through the shops until something caught Colette's eye.

"**Stop, stop, stop!**" she squeaked, and rushed into a store crammed with colorful fabric.

"What are these **beauties**?!"

"I thought you might find this part interesting," Latifah said, smiling. "These fabrics are decorated using the ancient **batik*** technique. Do you like them?"

"Do I **like** them? I **love**—" Colette started to say, until her **attention** was caught by a rack of blouses made of brocade and embellished with embroidery.

"OOOOHHH! WHAT ARE THESE?"

*Batik is a special technique that uses wax and dye to color fabric.

"These are called **KeBayas**. They are traditional clothing worn by Malaysian women," explained Ramlee. He picked up a long, brightly colored piece of cloth from another rack, and added, "This is a sarong. It's worn together with the kebaya. The sarong is wrapped around the waist to create

Look over there!

a long, tube-shaped skirt."

"My mom has some beautiful **KEBAYAS** for important events, and I have one, too," said Latifah. "I think they also look **GREAT** with a wide skirt, or even jeans!"

Colette turned to her friends with a serious look on her snout. "I know that we still have a lot more to **SEE**," she said. "But right now, can we take a break? Because I **can't** leave here without trying on some of these fabumouse clothes!"

Everyone burst out **laughing**. "I was hoping you would say that!" Latifah said. "I thought a chapter devoted to fashion would work for readers of the blog!"

Ramlee turned to the other Thea Sisters. "Why don't you all try some on?" he suggested. "I could take some photos for the blog!"

After their PHOTO SHOOT, the mice said farewell to Central Market. They walked over to a dazzling GREEN park in the center of a square. Overlooking the square was a large building with arched windows and shiny copper domes.

"Here we are in Merdeka Square! And

Say cheese!

that is the Sultan Abdul Samad Building," announced Latifah.

"Wow!" said Nicky, looking around. "This looks like a soccer field."

"Actually, a CRICKET pitch," Ramlee replied. "That's exactly what this space was used for in the past!"

"I'd love to play a game here!" Nicky said.

"Even just talking about sports is making

They used to play cricket here!

me hungry! How about we find a **snack**?" Pam suggested.

"Great idea," Latifah said. "Our next stop will be right up your alley!"

TABLES AND AROMAS

When the group arrived at the **next stop** on their Kuala Lumpur tour, Pam squeaked with delight.

"**Holey cheese!** This entire street is devoted to food!"

"Exactly!" Latifah said, winking at her friend. "Welcome to Jalan Alor!"

JALAN ALOR

Ready for a snack?

"In the restaurants and STALLS on this street, you can sample some of the **tastiest** Malaysian specialties," Ramlee said.

"I believe it! There are so many tables — and it all **smells** delicious!" remarked Nicky.

"Squeaking of smells . . ." said Violet, wrinkling her snout. "What's that strong one I'm getting?"

"It's coming from that stand down there," said Ramlee, pointing. "It's the smell of durian, also known as the **KING OF FRUITS**!"

The mouselets walked over to the display of durians: large oval fruits covered with tough spiny rinds. Paulina and Nicky decided to buy one and try its buttery flesh.

"**Yummm . . . delicious!**" Paulina squeaked

after having a taste. "It reminds me a little of a **creamy custard**."

"I wouldn't say that at all," Nicky added. "It tastes more like **creamy onions** to me!"

Latifah laughed. "With durian, you either **love** it or you **hate** it!"

Just then the mice noticed that Pam had **wandered away**. She was in front of a **STAND** where a pair of street vendors were preparing flatbread, and she seemed to be mesmerized.

The rodent holding Pam's attention wasn't the cook tending the **PAN**, but the mouse behind him, who was dexterously shaping balls of dough.

"Look!" Pam exclaimed as her friends approached. "It's a little like the way my dad and Vince work **pizza dough**, but instead of twirling the dough in the air, she turns each dough ball on the table and spreads it out until it becomes **PAPER-THIN**."

"Good eye, Pam!" Ramlee said. "You've just described the technique for making roti canai, one of our favorite snacks!"

Pam **OBSERVED** the vendors for a moment longer, then turned to Ramlee and Latifah.

"Would you please ask if I can take a video with my **MousePhone**? I would love to try making roti canai at home. If I record it, I can study their movements."

Latifah and **Ramlee** approached the mouse to ask, then returned to Pam.

"She said that she's very **happy** you are interested in learning to cook one of our traditional dishes," Latifah said. "She wants to do something she **NEVER** does . . . let you try rolling out the roti canai dough yourself!"

Pam didn't have to be told twice! She dove right in!

They all sampled the scrumptious snack,

along with **teh tarik**, a drink made with black tea and condensed milk. **Yum!**

Then the mice got back on track. Destination: Petronas Twin Towers!

"These twin skyscrapers are some of the **TALLEST** buildings in the world," Latifah said.

First, the group went up to the double-decker bridge that connects the towers, on the forty-first and forty-second floors.

"**SLIMY SWISS CHEESE!** What a view!" Colette exclaimed. The sun was setting, and the city spread beneath them.

"Wait until you see the observatory on the eighty-sixth floor!" Ramlee said.

The mouse was right. From the **top** of the tower, it was a *spectacular* show as **LIGHTS** came on throughout Kuala Lumpur. The Thea Sisters were squeakless!

"Well, **what do you think** of the tour so

far?" asked Ramlee on the way back down
to ground level. "Do you think our readers
will like our guide?"

"Not only will your readers **love** it,"
Colette assured him, "they'll never want it to
end!"

"Actually, we have one last stop before
we're done for the day . . ." Latifah said with
a mysterious smile.

"What is it?" asked Paulina, intrigued.

"Follow us, and you'll find out!" replied Ramlee, heading toward the park at the base of the two towers.

"Look! Is that water?" said Nicky.

"Do you hear music?" asked Violet.

"It's the dancing fountains of Lake Symphony!" Latifah squeaked.

Jets of water illuminated in a rainbow of colors rose to the rhythm of the music. The Thea Sisters lingered to admire Kuala Lumpur — a city that had already

captured their HEARTS!

THE ADVENTURE BEGINS!

The following morning, when the sky was still **DARK** and dotted with stars, the Thea Sisters climbed into a minivan with Latifah, Ramlee, and Safiq. It was time for the most adventurous part of the entire trip: exploring the unspoiled nature of Peninsular Malaysia, in the tropical rainforest of Taman Negara National Park.

But before that, a special stop was planned for Nicky, who loved outdoor sports. She was excited — and nervous — to climb GUNUNG LEDANG, also known as Mount Ophir.

They started *driving* south. After a few hours, they veered onto a long road that led to the entrance of Gunung Ledang National Park. The sky was beginning to get **BRiGHt**. In the *distance*, the mouselets spied mountains shrouded in a light fog. When they arrived at the **START** of the trail up Mount Ophir, the mice agreed it was the perfect time for a snack of *kuih bingka ubi*, a **tasty tapioca cake**. - - - - - - - - - - →

While studying the map at the trailhead, Nicky heard someone clearing his throat behind her.

"Um, excuse me . . ."

Nicky turned and found herself snout-to-snout with a mouse with brown fur. He seemed **friendly**.

"H-hi," the mouse stammered. "My name

is Didier. Are you and your friends CLIMBING Mount Ophir?" He explained that he had traveled from Belgium to join a group organized in Malaysia. But his trip got off to a bad start. He missed his flight and was delayed a couple of days. He had arrived in **Kuala Lumpur** two days after

Hi, my name is Didier...

his fellow travelers — and found that the group had left without him!

"So now I'm **trying** to make the best of the time I have here. I want to see the country on my own," Didier continued. "But I need a **guide** for this trail. Since you have one, I was thinking that maybe—"

"**ABSOLUTELY NOT!**" Safiq interrupted as he approached with the rest of the group. "There are already too many of us, and I have no intention of babysitting anyone!"

"But without us, he'll have to skip Mount Ophir!" Pam protested.

Ramlee tried to calm him. "I understand your concerns, Safiq, but all of us are experienced hikers. We **assure** you that if Didier needs help, we will be the ones helping him."

Safiq looked at Didier, then shrugged.

"As you wish," he grumbled. "But that means that if he decides to stop because he's tired, you'll be the ones to miss out on CLIMBING all the way up to the top!"

"Don't worry," whispered Colette to Didier. "I'm sure you'll make it!"

Colette proved to be right — at least at first. With backpacks and boots on, they started on their hike. They would ascend over four thousand feet to the top of Mount Ophir!

The trail soon became STEEP, and Didier found himself trailing the group.

"I'm sorry if I'm slowing you down. I haven't caught up on my sleep yet," Didier confided. "Since arriving in Malaysia, I keep getting confused about directions and end up getting so delayed that it's already morning by the time I arrive to the place I should've slept, but I didn't want to waste any more time!"

"Don't worry," Pam reassured him. "We're not in a hurry. I'm sure the view will be just as good even if we arrive an hour later than planned!"

But despite the encouragement of his new friends, Didier was still having a hard time. Agile Safiq led the group up the trail, which became trickier. At some points, the mice had to climb STEEP wooden steps, and at others, they had to clamber up the rock face with only a rope for support!

You can do it!

It's so hard . . .

"I can't do it!" Didier puffed, his cheeks as pink as a cat's tongue. He craned his neck toward the top of the rock they were climbing. "Look how high that is!"

"I told you this would happen!" Safiq said, shaking his snout.

Latifah gave the guide a dirty look and moved *CLOSER* to Didier.

"Don't listen to him," she said, putting a paw on his shoulder. "I don't know what's got his whiskers twisted up. I'm sure **YOU CAN DO IT**. Don't think about how far you have to go — only think about the next pawstep you're going to take."

"Will that really help?" Didier asked.

"It's always **worked** for me!" Latifah smiled.

"And just think," Colette said, "once we get to the top, you can finally sit down and

take a load off your paws."

Didier took her advice to heart. Together, the whole group reached the top of Mount Ophir!

A LEGEND TO DREAM ABOUT

"How spectacular!" exclaimed Nicky as she admired the lush GREEN landscape below.

"It could just be the mist, but it looks like it's right out of a fairy tale," remarked Violet.

"Or a LEGEND . . ." Ramlee smiled. "An ancient legend, known throughout Malaysia, was born near here."

Latifah jumped right in. "It is said that on this mountain lived a PRINCESS who was separated from her beloved prince, who lived on Mount Rundok . . ."

She told them the rest of the legend. The two sweethearts were victims of an evil curse that kept them apart, and the only time they could be together was at night, when the peak of Mount Rundok would *LEAN* toward the peak of Mount Ophir.

"It is said that the reason the top of Mount Rundok is **inclined** toward Mount Ophir today is in memory of the couple," Latifah concluded.

"Oh, what a **romantic** story!" Colette sighed dreamily.

A light rain began to fall.

"The bad weather shouldn't last long," Safiq said as he studied the clouds. "We can start the climb down soon."

"Oh n-n-no!" stammered Didier. "I was so focused on *CLIMBING UP* that I didn't think about **climbing back down**!"

Latifah winked at the sad Belgian tourist.

"At the end, there's a **reward** waiting for

you! Let's make like a cheese wheel and roll!"

The reward she was referring to was not far from where the Thea Sisters and their friends had met Didier: PUTERI FALLS!

After walking down a rough staircase carved into the rocks, the mice admired the waterfall, which flowed into natural pools below. Then they returned to their minivan.

"Thank you for allowing me to join you on this **excursion**," said Didier. "If I hadn't met you, I would never have seen the view from Mount Ophir's summit, and I would never have known the legend of the princess. And most of all, I would never have discovered that I'm able to climb the side of a mountain using only a rope!"

"It was a real pleasure having you with us," said Paulina. "What are you doing next?"

"I don't know for sure. Maybe if I stop

missing all my trains and buses, I could catch up with my group," answered Didier. He **LOOKED** around sadly, and said, "Well, have a nice trip!"

Latifah, Ramlee, and the Thea Sisters watched Didier walk away with his snout down.

It's an exceptional place!

It's beautiful!

What a view!

Paulina broke the **silence**. "Please tell me you're all thinking what I'm thinking!"

Everyone nodded.

"Didieeeer! **Wait** up!" Ramlee called after him.

"**WHAT HAPPENED?** Did I leave something behind?" asked the mouse, embarrassed.

Come with us!

Nicky shook her head. "No, it's just that your GROUP can't continue their trip without you!"

Didier looked around, confused. "My group?! Where?"

"Right here!" Ramlee smiled. "We're ready to leave on our next adventure!"

You're part of our group!

ON THE JUNGLE TRAIN!

Although he was a less **adventurous** mouse than his new friends, Didier was now part of their group! His presence gave the two **BLOGGER** friends an idea: They could ask for his perspective and use it in their guidebook under **"TIPS FOR THE LESS-EXPERIENCED TRAVELER."**

The mice were waiting beneath an awning at Gemas train station, a **small** village not far from Gunung Ledang National Park. Didier told Latifah, "The most challenging part of the ascent up Mount Ophir for me was definitely the climb with the **ropes**."

Latifah nodded as she took **notes**. "And if you did it again, is there anything you didn't have today that you would take with you next time?"

"Hmm . . . a pair of climbing GLOVES. Then I would have had a better grip and would have felt more secure on the hardest spots," Didier answered.

Soon a short train puffed into the station. The group scurried aboard quicker than a gerbil on a wheel. This **train** would travel all N*GHT through the forest, taking them to Taman Negara National Park!

What would you bring with you?

Gloves!

As soon as the train began to move, Pam held out a small bag to her friends.

"There was a food stand outside the station selling a

local specialty: **nasi lemak**. I bought some for everybody!" she said.

Pam began distributing the nasi lemak, little pyramids of rice cooked in coconut milk and served with eggs and **spicy sauce**. A jolt from the train made her lurch as she was pawing one to Latifah, whose heavy backpack rolled onto it.

"Oh no! Your nasi lemak is completely crushed!" exclaimed Pam.

"Here, Latifah, **take mine**," Didier offered.

"Thank you, but I don't want you to give up your food," Latifah answered, a bit sad.

"I'm not hungry! Really!" Didier insisted. "I'm happy to give you my nasi lemak."

"Okay," Latifah said, giving in. "What if we split yours and mine? That way we each get half of the squashed one and half of the good one!"

"Done!" Didier nodded, **blushing**. He sat next to Latifah and divided the rice with her.

From her seat in the bunk above them, Colette **smiled**. "Well, that was very nice of them," she whispered to Violet.

Violet nodded, giggling.

Soon, they all settled down for the night. The train sped into the darkness, past palm plantations and tiny villages, and lulled by its movement, everyone fell **asleep**.

At the first light of dawn, the train arrived at its destination: Jerantut.

"We still have a bit of travel to get to **TAMAN NEGARA**, but this is as close as the train comes to it," explained Safiq.

"Mousetastic!" Nicky said. "How will we get there?"

"We want to show the readers of our guide

an **adventure** full of many different things," Ramlee said. "And since we've traveled by car and by train, now

we'll go by boat!"

WELCOME TO THE JUNGLE!

The last leg of the journey to Taman Negara National Park was by far the most **memorable** for the Thea Sisters. After exiting Jerantut **TRAIN STATION,** the mice came to a little marina. They climbed onto a sampan, a tapered **WOODEN** boat, and started down the Tembeling River.

They sailed, making their way into the jungle. The **plant life** on the riverbank became taller and thicker, and the mouselets spotted **MULTICOLORED** birds and some water buffalo cooling off in shallower parts of the river.

Ramlee was enthusiastic about the plants and animals, and snapped lots of

TAMAN NEGARA

Taman Negara is the best-known national park in Malaysia. It occupies **more than 1,600 square miles** and is home to one of the planet's most ancient tropical rainforests, estimated to be 130 million years old! Many **thousands** of species of plants and animals live in the park.

PHOTOS to use in the travel guide.

When they arrived in **TAMAN NEGARA**, Safiq took care of getting the entry tickets and permits. Meanwhile, before beginning their jungle adventure, the rest of the mice decided to treat themselves to some steaming noodles and fried rice from a restaurant floating by the riverbank.

When the group finally entered the park, Nicky couldn't contain her excitement.

"We're in one of the oldest rainforests on the planet!" she exclaimed.

"There is a bit of a **hike** to where we will set up camp," Safiq said. "Let's get moving!"

They took a path through the jungle. They admired the huge trees with **roots** above the soil and listened carefully to the sounds made by animals that quickly scurried away to hide from them.

"There are a l-l-lot of animals living in this forest!" whispered Didier, who flinched at every noise.

"Exactly! Hundreds of species of birds, monkeys, deer, wild boar, elephants . . ." Safiq said, moving **confidently** down the trail. When he realized Didier was a little afraid of all the **WILDLIFE**, he continued in a menacing voice, "And rhinos, tigers, leopards, bears . . ."

Didier gulped. "They **ALL** l-live here?"

"Yes, but don't worry," Paulina assured him. "The animals **fear** you more than you fear them because they don't know you. It's very **unlikely** that any will come toward you!"

The mice soon arrived at the sheltered clearing that would serve as their campsite for their expedition.

"Shall we gather some **WOOD** to light a campfire?" Nicky suggested.

"Good idea. Let's ask Safiq what kind would be best," **Ramlee** agreed, looking around for their guide. "Hey! Where did he go?"

"He went *that way*," Violet said, pointing toward the **river** flowing nearby.

"I think he was talking on the phone."

"How is that possible?" Paulina wondered. "There's no cell reception in the park . . ."

"Our MousePhones are out of range here," Ramlee explained. "But he has a **satellite phone** that gets reception. Still, he shouldn't have just left . . ."

"It's okay. We can figure out collecting

Where's Safiq?

Strange . . .

He was on the phone . . .

firewood ourselves," Nicky said. She could tell Ramlee was upset by Safiq's behavior. "We won't go far. **Who's coming with me?**"

Didier glanced at Latifah, then volunteered uncertainly. "M-me?"

Nicky and Didier began to scour the surrounding area for DRY branches.

"Do you feel a little better about the animals?" asked Nicky.

"A **little**," Didier said. "The most wildlife I've ever been exposed to are tiny spiders and lizards . . ."

"Hmm . . . so when I tell you that I see a lizard a bit **BIGGER** than the ones you're used to, you won't be scared, right?" Nicky asked, pointing at a large varan peeking out from the bushes, flicking its tongue.

"That's m-more than SLIGHTLY bigger!"

Didier squeaked — and highTailed it back to their camp!

"You're back already?" Latifah asked, surprised.

"Yep!" Nicky said, giving an understanding LOOK to Didier, who was red-faced and panting. "We . . . er . . . had a race to see who could get to the campsite first."

As the group finished putting up the TENTS, the sun was beginning to set. They ate dinner and chatted. It was their first night in the jungle, and they were as excited as a rat with a vat of fondue.

Heeeelp!

"How about we go around the circle and each say what we hope to see on our **TAMAN NEGARA** adventure?" Colette suggested.

Everyone's answers varied, from butterflies to thousand-year-old trees to **waterfalls**. When it was Latifah's turn, everyone went silent. She'd already seen so many things, this would be interesting.

"I really want to see a rafflesia," the mouselet said.

"What's that?" Violet asked.

"The biggest flower in the world!" Latifah explained. "I would love to include a

P H O T O of it in our guide."

"I'm sure we'll find one!" Didier said, smiling at her.

"I think so, too," Colette agreed.

"And now, it's time to say good night." Ramlee yawned. "Tomorrow we hunt for Latifah's rafflesia!"

I'd like to find a rafflesia . . .

A PLUNGE INTO NATURE

At the first light of **Dawn** the next morning, the campsite was crawling with activity. Now that they'd made it to TAMAN NEGARA, the Thea Sisters and their friends were impatient to head out into the jungle, and none of them wanted to waste time sleeping.

"I'm ready! Are you?" Ramlee asked as he hung **binoculars** around his neck.

"We are!" Colette replied.

"But we **won't be able** to go very far without Safiq . . ." Violet said. They all **LOOKED** around for the guide.

"Don't tell me he's on the phone again!" Latifah scowled.

"I think he is," Nicky said as she strained to see him in the distance.

Without another squeak, Ramlee scampered off. He returned a few minutes later with Safiq.

"Everything okay?" Latifah asked, noticing Ramlee's frown.

"Everything's fine," he answered quickly. "Let's get GOING. We've already wasted enough time."

As the mice began to hike, they turned their focus to the wonders of the rainforest they were in. Safiq pointed out many exotic plants and strange insects around them.

Everything okay?

"Our **first stop** is the canopy walkway: a bridge suspended high up between trees of the forest," Safiq said.

"**CHEESE NIBLETS!** I can't wait!" exclaimed Pam.

"Me neither!" added Nicky. "I read that the **BRIDGE** is more than one hundred twenty feet above the ground!"

After crossing the bridge, the mice traveled to Lata Berkoh Falls by taking a boat up the Tahan River. They enjoyed the **ARCHES** of greenery formed by trees rising above the river and admired the ferns and orchids surrounding it.

When the group reached Lubuk Simpon, a natural pool along the river with a grassy bank, they agreed to *relax* for a bit.

"This is the perfect spot for a picnic," Colette declared.

"Safiq, can we swim here?" asked Nicky.

The guide examined the calm waters and nodded.

Nicky cheered. "How about we cool off before we EAT?"

The mouselets didn't waste any time: They immediately jumped in!

As they lounged in the water, Latifah said, "Today I took so many notes for our travel guide that I filled up the notebook I had with me!"

"Awesome!" Ramlee squeaked as he joined his friends in the river. "I'm very happy with all the photos I took."

Paulina smiled. "I also took a lot of **PHOTOS** — they'll be a fabumouse memory of this trip!"

Just then Paulina noticed that Colette, who was standing by some **rocks** a few feet away, was surrounded by **COLORFUL** butterflies.

"Stay as still as petrified Parmesan!" Paulina called to her friend. "This is a photo op that **CAN'T BE MISSED**. I'll get my camera!"

Paulina got out of the water and **scurried** to the clearing where the group had left their backpacks. To her surprise, she saw Didier.

"**Oh! Paulina, it's you!**" he exclaimed, quickly zipping his backpack shut.

"Of course it's me! I came to get my camera," Paulina said. "What are you doing? Aren't you coming with us for a **swim**?"

"Yes, yes, I'll be right

there! I was just . . . finishing something up," Didier answered. "**LET'S GO!** I'll follow you."

Paulina picked up her camera and **LED** the way for Didier, but not before giving a **suspicious** glance at his backpack.

CLUES!

SAFIQ KEEPS ANSWERING STRANGE PHONE CALLS AWAY FROM THE REST OF THE GROUP.

DIDIER HAD A STRANGE REACTION TO PAULINA ARRIVING IN THE CLEARING.

ARE THEY EACH HIDING SOMETHING?

missing!

The best end to a day spent *exploring* nature is nestling into a cozy sleeping bag, listening to the insects chirping. With their hearts full from the day's wonders and their legs tired from the miles walked, sleep came easily to the mouselets.

The next morning, after a NIGHT of restful sleep, Paulina opened her eyes feeling energized and ready to *explore*. She saw that Nicky was still *asleep*, and she didn't hear any noise outside the tent, so she figured she must be the only one awake.

Ready to start the new day, Paulina scribbled a note and placed it on top of her sleeping bag as she left the tent. She decided to take a quick **WALK** along the nearby riverbank, but she didn't want her friends to worry about her when they woke up.

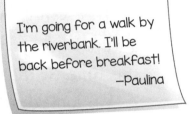

I'm going for a walk by the riverbank. I'll be back before breakfast!
—Paulina

The mouselet strolled slowly, breathing the fresh morning air and enjoying the birds chirping and the blue sky that peeked through the **TALL** trees. When she was almost back to the campsite, Latifah's voice startled her.

"Ramlee! Where are you?!"

Paulina quickened her pace. When she got to the tents, she found that the other Thea Sisters, Latifah, and Didier were up. They all seemed very worried.

"Ramlee is missing," Latifah announced when she saw Paulina.

"**Missing?! Are you sure?**" Paulina

asked, surprised. "Could he have gone for a walk, too?"

Nicky shook her head. "Latifah said he always leaves a NOTE, like you did. But this time, he didn't!"

"We looked for him around here," Pam

said. "And we obviously can't reach him on his cell phone."

"What does Safiq say?" asked Paulina. "Where is he?"

The mice realized that **no one** had seen their guide that morning. They went to his tent and called out to him, but no one answered.

"That's **strange**," said Pam. She raised a corner of the tent flap to **PEER** inside. "What in the name of string cheese?!"

"What is it?" asked Latifah.

"**SAFIQ IS GONE, TOO!** And so is all of his stuff!" Pam said, throwing the tent flap open.

Colette frowned. "He must have packed up his gear and left!"

After this unsettling discovery, the mice decided to check through Ramlee's tent more carefully.

"Everything seems to be in place," said Pam.

"I think the only thing missing is his binoculars. The rest is still all here," Latifah confirmed. "But wait — he left his camera behind. That's odd, he usually takes it **everywhere**!"

"Everything looks a bit messy. It seems like he left in a hurry, convinced he would be right back," said Nicky.

"Yes, but where could he have gone alone, abruptly, and with only binoculars?" asked Violet, **PERPLEXED**.

Paulina frowned again. "This doesn't seem right. Both mice are **missing** — but it seems like only Safiq planned to leave!"

"**What is going on?**" Latifah wrung her paws, worried. "**Where did they go?**"

A moment of silence followed those

questions. It was suddenly interrupted by Didier, who had stayed quiet through their whole search.

"I THINK . . . I CAN HELP YOU!"

A DANGEROUS ATTEMPT!

The Thea Sisters and Latifah all stared at the mouse, confused.

"Didier, do you know what might have happened to Ramlee and Safiq?" Pam asked.

"Well, I did hear something," he began.

The mouse told them that shortly before dawn, he WOKE UP because of hushed sounds from outside his tent.

"At first, I thought it was an animal," he explained. "But now I'm realizing that it could have been Ramlee's and Safiq's pawsteps!"

"That's possible," Latifah said. She was clearly CONCERNED. "Do you have any idea which **direction** they went?"

Didier hesitated a moment and then said, "I — I *think so*. As I was lying in my tent, the sound seemed to be **moving away** behind me. So I think they went . . . that way!"

Let's find them!

They went that way . . .

The Thea Sisters and Latifah turned in the direction he **pointed**. It was a dense area of forest. Unlike the heavily beaten paths the group had walked on elsewhere in the JUNGLE, there was only a very faint trail. Nevertheless, the friends did not hesitate and scampered to get their backpacks ready to go search for Ramlee and Safiq.

Soon Didier was leading the group through thick plants.

"We've been walking for quite a while," Colette remarked. "Do you think we're going in the right direction?"

"I think I hear the sound of water," said Latifah, quickly moving into the lead and heading into the BRUSH. "Maybe we are coming to a riv — **AAAAHHH! HEEEELP!**"

"Latifah!" Nicky cried. She sprinted

forward as her friend started **Slipping** down a steep bank that had been hidden by the brush.

Luckily, Nicky's reflexes were quick, and she was able to **GRAB** Latifah before she fell toward the **stream**.

Colette helped Latifah over to the base of a large tree to help her recover from her frightening accident.

Heeeelp!

"Didier, for the love of cheese, do you really think that Ramlee and Safiq could have gone **through** here?" Colette asked. "We can't even get through!"

Didier blushed to the roots of his fur, and **LOOKED** uncertainly from Latifah to the Thea Sisters.

Here's some water... "I — I think so," he finally said.

Then he took off his backpack, opened it, and took out his water bottle.

"Here, Latifah. If you drink a little ᴡᴀᴛᴇʀ, you'll feel a lot bett —"

But Didier was interrupted by Latifah, who sprang up from where she was sitting, grabbed his backpack, and took out a pair of binoculars. Staring at him coldly, she asked, "And where did you get these?!"

CLUES!
WHY DOES DIDIER ALWAYS SEEM UNCERTAIN WHEN GIVING DETAILS ABOUT RAMLEE AND SAFIQ'S DISAPPEARANCE?

AND WHY DOES LATIFAH THINK DIDIER HAS BINOCULARS THAT DON'T BELONG TO HIM?

IT'S NOT WHAT IT LOOKS LIKE!

The Thea Sisters were squeakless. Didier blushed even more red and fixed his gaze on the **binoculars** Latifah had taken from his backpack.

Finally, it was Colette who asked, "Are those . . . Ramlee's binoculars?"

"Yes," confirmed Latifah, showing them the shoulder strap. "I gave this strap to him — **GREEN** is his favorite color."

I can explain . . .

"It — it's not what it looks like . . ." Didier said. Everyone stared at him skeptically.

Paulina sighed, disappointed. She didn't like getting Didier in

trouble, but it was time to clear up the situation.

"Didier, those **binoculars** don't belong to you," she said. "And I think I know when you took them: yesterday when we were swimming."

"Yesterday? What are you talking about?" asked Violet.

"Remember when I went to get my **camera** to photograph Colette with the butterflies?" Paulina said. "When I got over to our backpacks, I had the feeling Didier was **hiding** something in his."

Nicky faced Didier. **"Is that true?"**

He nodded in silence.

"Why did you **steal** Ramlee's binoculars?" Latifah demanded. **"What are you hiding from us?"**

Didier found the courage to squeak.

What are you hiding?

"Wait! I didn't *steal* the binoculars! Please believe me! I promise I had nothing to do with Ramlee's disappearance!"

"Okay, then **explain** what happened," Pam said.

"I asked Ramlee to borrow his **binoculars**," explained Didier. "But Paulina is right about everything else. When she saw me by the river, I quickly **HID** them in my backpack. I didn't want her to find them — or rather, I didn't want **Latifah** to find them."

Latifah was surprised. She frowned and asked, "Why?"

"You wanted to see a rafflesia, so I was going to try to find one for you," confessed Didier, embarrassed.

Violet cut in. "And you thought that the binoculars could help you do that."

"Yes. I wanted to **impress** Latifah by finding a rafflesia," Didier continued, blushing. "And for the same reason, I told you that I knew which **direction** Ramlee and Safiq had gone."

You can borrow them!

Thank you. You're very kind!

"So you actually never heard a noise?" Pam asked, wincing.

"Well . . . I did hear **NOISE**, but I'm not sure they went in this direction," Didier admitted. "I lied because I wanted Latifah to think I was clever and **adventurous**. Instead, I only made us all waste precious time and almost made Latifah end up in the **river**. And now I seem even more like a cheesebrain than I did before. I am so sorry. Please forgive me."

We can't lose any more time!

"Well, you did lead us down the wrong path when we really need to find Ramlee," Colette said, annoyed. "But I suppose you were trying to make Latifah's wish come true."

Latifah considered Didier with a scowl, then finally sighed and nodded. "Of course," she said. "But you have to promise to stop lying. Friends don't lie to friends. Plus, we don't have any time to lose. We have to figure out what happened to Ramlee!"

A PROMISING CLUE

After Didier's confession, the Thea Sisters were pretty sure that the trail they were on would not lead them to Ramlee.

"There's only one thing to do: We have to start over from where they left!" Nicky said. So the group returned to the campsite. Meanwhile, Latifah tried Ramlee's phone again.

"It's useless. There's just no signal here," the mouselet said, disappointed.

"We'll try again later," said Paulina. "Right now, let's look for new CLUES that can give us a new plan."

"They couldn't have disappeared into thin air!" Colette remarked.

"Let's roll up our sleeves and examine the area," Paulina said, starting to **LOOK** around again. "There must be **SOMETHING** we missed!"

The mice immediately set to work combing through the tents of their two missing companions, then extended their search to the rest of the campsite and the surrounding area. Finally, they found a clue.

Check it out!

"I think I found something over here!" Pam announced. She was crouched near the shore of the stream flowing by their camp.

"Pawprints!" Nicky exclaimed. She studied the muddy ground.

"Even better: two

sets of pawprints!" Paulina said. "Here's the first set, and here's the second. These tell us that Safiq and Ramlee passed through here a short distance from each other."

"Then where did they go?" Colette wondered aloud.

To answer that question, the mouselets followed the footprints to the start of a *trail* they had never been on. The muddy ground by the water gave way to dry dirt covered by forest plant life, and the **tracks** became spottier.

"We've got to follow this trail to try to find Ramlee," Pam began, when **SUDDENLY** the reflection of a silvery object peeking through some leaves by the path caught her attention.

"Crusty carburetors! This is –"

"Ramlee's phone!" Latifah cried. She ran over to it.

"It won't turn on," Pam said, pushing the **POWER** button several times. "And the screen is cracked."

"Maybe he dropped it while he was walking," Colette said.

But Violet was not CONVINCED. "It's strange. There's no cell signal in the park. Why would he have his phone out?"

"Hold on, mouselets," Paulina said. She had the **phone** in her paws and was

It's Ramlee's . . .

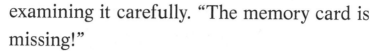

examining it carefully. "The memory card is missing!"

"This is becoming even **stranger**!" said Nicky.

"The only way to get answers is to find Ramlee," said Pam.

The group returned to their campsite to grab their backpacks and continue their search.

"Are you all set, Didier?" asked Violet when everyone else was ready to leave. "Shall we go?"

"**I'M NOT COMING**," he answered firmly.

"Why?" asked Colette.

"Because without me slowing you down, your search will be *FASTER*," Didier explained. "And more important, because someone needs to be here in case Ramlee comes back."

Latifah was moved by how thoughtful Didier was, and smiled at him gratefully. "Thank you, Didier!" she said.

CLUES!

RAMLEE'S PHONE WAS FOUND ON THE TRAIL NOT FAR FROM THE CAMPSITE—AND ITS MEMORY CARD IS MISSING. HOW DID THE PHONE GET THERE, AND WHERE DID THE MEMORY CARD GO?

STRONGER THAN ANY OBSTACLE!

After saying good-bye to Didier, the Thea Sisters left the campsite, determined to find out what had happened. What worried the mouselets the most was the thought of their friend alone in the jungle.

"Safiq had a plan to leave, since he took all the necessary gear," Paulina mused.

"But Ramlee must have gone in a hurry, since he left everything behind in his tent," added Nicky.

The six mouselets hiked cautiously through the rainforest. Together, they felt like they could face any obstacle. But soon, the group found the trail blocked by an enormouse fallen TREE TRUNK.

"In the forest, this is the equivalent of a **STOP** sign!" Pam joked.

Nicky STUDIED the trunk to see if it was possible to go around it, but the brush was too thick on both sides of the trail.

"Come on, mouselets! It'll take more than a tree trunk to stop us!" Paulina squeaked.

This isn't good!

"Let's **CLIMB OVER IT** and move on!"

"**Yes!**" Latifah agreed. "There's no time to lose. We have to find Ramlee!"

She placed her paws on the slippery BARK and tried to get over the trunk with one big jump.

"Ooouuuch!" she squeaked a moment later.

"**Are you okay?**" Violet asked, running over.

"No! I'm not okay! I hurt my wrist . . ."

Shall we go over it?

Latifah said, cradling the **wounded** arm. Then she covered her face with her paws and began to cry. "And we still haven't found Ramlee!"

The **THEA SISTERS** looked at one another.

"You know what?" said Colette. "This trunk is not going anywhere. Let's sit and reenergize for a few minutes. Soon we'll be jumping over the trunk like kangaroo mice!"

The mouselet took out her *water bottle* and some granola bars and passed them around to her friends. The short rest helped Latifah calm down.

"Do you want to know what I call Ramlee?" Latifah said with a smile. **"Sloth!"**

"Sloth? Like the slowest animal in the world?" asked Colette.

"That's right. On our travels, I don't stay

still for a second! But he loves to take it easy, to take in the sights, to find the best light for his photo . . ."

"That explains the keychain hanging on your backpack!" Colette exclaimed, pointing.

"Exactly!" Latifah nodded. "Ramlee

We needed a rest!

Thanks!

Delicious!

Here!

gave it to me. It's become our mascot when we travel!"

A moment later, Latifah got up with a bounce. "I don't know about you, but I'm feeling fully recharged and ready to *MOVE ON*!" she squeaked.

DARKNESS
FALLS . . .

Paulina looked down at her watch and **sighed**. This was harder than finding a cheese crumb in a haystack. They had been walking for hours and had found nothing but more wild **nature**. There was still no trace of Ramlee.

"Ramlee!" shouted Colette as she climbed a natural staircase formed by the gnarled tree **roots**.

"Ramlee!" echoed Latifah.

The only answer was the chirping of the birds in the branches above them.

"It's okay. We'll keep **SEARCHING** for him," Nicky declared. "We've covered a lot of area. We can't **GIVE UP NOW**!"

"Agreed . . . but the sun will be setting soon," Violet pointed out. "We have to start looking for somewhere safe to spend the NIGHT."

Colette pointed her snout upward. "Vi is right. The light is beginning to fade . . ."

When the six mouselets had left the campsite in a hurry that morning, they'd grabbed their sleeping bags, but they hadn't thought they'd have to spend the night in the **heart** of the jungle — especially not without a tent.

"Don't worry,"

Uh-oh!

The sun is setting . . .

Latifah said. "There are several shelters for hikers in the park. We'll figure out which is the closest and head for it right away."

Paulina looked at the map. "If I have our location correct, there should be a shelter just east of here, **NOT TOO**

It's getting dark . . .

There are shelters!

FAR. So we need to go . . . that way!"

The mouselets hiked down the path, feeling hopeful. The sun was **SETTING** and the sky had turned beautiful shades of pink and purple, when they finally reached a small grassy clearing.

"That's like something a TRAPEZE ARTIST would use!" Nicky said, looking in astonishment at a building standing high among the trees on wooden stilts.

"We did it!" rejoiced Latifah. "This is a **BUMBUN**!"

"A bum-what?" repeated Pam.

"Of course!" Paulina said, smiling. "I read about this **online**. These shelters were built to be a safe place for visitors to observe animals up close without scaring them, especially at night! We should be able to climb right up."

"And **tonight**, they have another very special purpose," Pam said, relieved. "To provide a good night of sleep to six

mice on a mission!"

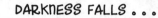

A NiGHT iN THE JUNGLE

Finding the shelter before it got **DARK** lifted the spirits of the Thea Sisters and Latifah. They could sleep in a safe place, which meant they would be well rested to resume their **SEARCH** the next day.

"This is a surprise!" exclaimed Paulina when she entered the cabin and saw four **bunk beds**. "I didn't know the bumbuns had furniture!"

"It's so **VISITORS** who spend the night here can get a little rest while waiting to **SEE** the wildlife," explained Latifah as she arranged her sleeping bag on one of the top bunks.

"Do you think we'll see any **animals**?" asked Violet, excited at the prospect.

"I think so," answered Paulina. "Wild animals have an **intense** nightlife. And we are deep in the jungle — their home!"

As the mouselets set up their beds, the sky got darker, and stars twinkled through the trees. After a quick dinner, they studied the park **MAP** by the light of their flashlights.

"We're here, and we've already searched this entire **AREA**," Nicky said, making a circle on the map. "Tomorrow, I say we continue along this trail and go to this region. What do you think?"

"I think it's a good plan," agreed Pam.

Latifah looked out the window and

sighed. "Let's hope Ramlee also has a safe place to spend the NIGHT . . ."

"Ramlee is used to adapting to less-than-comfortable conditions while traveling, just like you are," Colette assured her. "I'm sure that—"

FRRRR! FRRRR! FRRRRR! FRRRR!

What was that noise? The mouselets strained their ears to listen better.

"Did you hear that strange rustling?" **whispered** Violet.

Without squeaking a word, Paulina nodded and signaled to her friends to **follow** her to the cabin's wide window.

"It's a **MALAY CIVET**!" whispered Latifah, excited.

"A civet? What's that?" asked Pam.

"It's a type of nocturnal mammal that mostly lives on the ground," explained Latifah.

It looked like a sort of striped ferret. It made the bushes *rustle* as it moved quickly from one to another.

The Malay civet was just the first **wild animal** that came close to the cabin that evening. Soon afterward, the mouselets caught a glimpse of a tapir and a deer!

Then the six friends began to **yawn** and decided it was best to settle into their bunks and try to get some sleep.

"Ramlee must have taken the most beautiful **PHOTOS** tonight," mused Violet as she got ready for bed.

Pam remained positive. "Well, that means we'll have to come back here with him once we—"

THUMP!

The mouselets froze.

"What is it this time?" Colette asked, jumping to her feet.

"I don't know," said Nicky. "But it seems to be coming from the stairs."

Did you hear that?

The mouselets were scared. Was it possible that an animal was climbing up the **stairs** of the shelter? And was it . . . dangerous?

The Thea Sisters and Latifah held on to one another and instinctively BACKED away, toward the corner of the room farthest from the entrance. They pointed their flashlights at the door. The sound came closer and closer. But none of them could ever have *imagined* what was about to come into the cabin.

The door swung open, and they saw . . . not a wild animal, but

the friend they had been searching for!

TOGETHER AGAIN

"Mouselets! **It's so nice to see you!**" Ramlee cried.

"**Ramlee!**" Latifah exclaimed, running to hug her friend. All the tension in the room gave way to happiness.

The Thea Sisters waited for the two **friends** to finish greeting each other and then scurried to welcome Ramlee.

Finally!

"How long have you been hiking?" Violet asked as she cleared a bunk for Ramlee.

"You must be so tired!"

"Are you hungry? We have some sandwiches, **chocolate**, and fruit!" offered Colette.

"I also have a clean towel and a sweatshirt you can borrow," added Nicky.

"Thank you all. You are very kind," said Ramlee, curling up in his bunk. His eyes were starting to droop. "I thought you might be LOOKING for me — and you have no idea how happy I was when I realized you weren't too far!"

"**How did you find us?**" Paulina asked. "Did you hear us call your name?"

"No. An old friend showed me . . ." Ramlee grinned and took a little wooden **sloth** out of his pocket.

Latifah's eyes opened wide. "My keychain! I didn't realize I'd lost it!"

Ramlee **told** them that shortly after leaving the campsite that morning, he realized he'd gotten lost in the JUNGLE. The more he tried to find his way back, the more he found himself going around in circles.

"At some point, though, I finally managed to take a different trail, and I found myself in front of a huge fallen tree trunk."

"The TRUNK where we stopped to rest this afternoon!" exclaimed Colette.

"Yes — because that's exactly where I found the sloth!" Ramlee smiled. "I realized that you couldn't be too far away. So I followed the path, and kept going even when NIGHT began to fall. Eventually I came to this shelter, and when I saw the glow of the flashlights inside, I figured you had to be here. I could have squeaked with joy, but I didn't want to scare any of the animals!"

"It was lucky that the Malay civet kept us awake!" said Nicky.

"We still have lots of **Questions** for you, Ramlee," Pam added.

Paulina jumped in. "Yes! Why did you leave the campsite without taking anything and without **telling** anyone? And do you

They must be nearby!

know where Saf . . ." She trailed off. Ramlee was sleeping like a baby mouseling, exhausted from his long day.

Pam chuckled. "I think we'll need to wait a bit longer to get the rest of our questions answered!"

"At least until morning," added Violet, yawning. She was a sleepysnout herself. "But for now, the most important thing is that we're all together again!"

A SERIOUS
SUSPICION

The night passed peacefully, and soon the morning sun shone in and woke the travelers in the **BUMBUN**. They picked up their conversation right where they'd left off.

"Here's your **phone**," Latifah said, pawing Ramlee the MousePhone she and the Thea Sisters had found the previous morning.

"We kept trying to call you, even though we knew there was no signal in the park," Paulina said.

"That was before we realized you'd lost it," added Colette.

Ramlee turned the phone over in his paw thoughtfully. "Actually, I didn't **lose** it," he said. "It was stolen!"

"Cheese on a stick! Stolen?!" Violet squeaked.

"Yes — by Safiq," Ramlee said. "And I was trying to get it **BACK** when I got as lost as a rat in a maze!"

Latifah and the Thea Sisters exchanged a **worried** look. They thought something strange had happened at the camp. Now they knew for sure!

"Okay, Ramlee, **TELL US** from the beginning exactly what happened yesterday," said Paulina.

He gathered his thoughts for a moment, then began. "Do you remember when I told you that Safiq was a very popular tour guide?"

"Yes," Nicky replied. "He said he was too busy to accompany us on this trip. But, later on, he called to say that he was free."

"Well, I don't think he ever wanted to help us and he just used this trip as an excuse to wander around the park undisturbed," Ramlee said.

"I did notice that Safiq was **unusual**," Latifah added. "He never seemed to have any interest in our TRIP, and he was constantly on the phone!"

"From the start, I was extremely annoyed

with Safiq's behavior," Ramlee said. "Then something happened yesterday that made me *suspect* that he had a secret!"

"Rancid ricotta! What happened?" Colette asked.

"When Safiq was **again** on the phone right as we were about to leave,

Hi, it's me . . .

On the phone again!

I got upset," Ramlee replied. "I wanted an explanation. But as I approached him, I overheard part of his phone call, and it left me stunned."

"**What was he saying?**" asked Pam.

"Something about a large quantity of TIMBER," Ramlee said. "It was to go through Malaysia and then be sold to other countries."

Latifah turned as PALE as mozzarella. "Are you saying that Safiq is a timber smuggler?"

"Wait a second," Nicky said. "If that's true, it's a very **serious** matter. Entire forests in Southeast Asia are illegally chopped down so that the timber can be sold abroad!"

"Some of the world's oldest forests are being DESTROYED," Paulina added. "It not only kills trees, but also takes away the

natural habitats of many types of plants and
animals!"

"It's terrible," Ramlee agreed. "I don't
think Safiq is an actual **smuggler**, but I

Are you sure?

That's a serious problem!

He was talking
about timber . . .

do think he's involved somehow."

"What does that have to do with us?" Violet frowned.

"I'm not sure. But yesterday, I realized that without meaning to, I had taken a video of Safiq while he was squeaking on the phone," Ramlee revealed. "I had been filming for material to use in a video for our guide."

"Then we have proof that he was involved in the plan to cut down the trees, right?" Colette asked hopefully. "What does Safiq say in the video?"

"I was only able to listen to a small part of it. I wanted to continue keeping my EYES OPEN and then tell all of you at the first opportunity," Ramlee went on. "But Safiq must have noticed me filming. Before he FLED in the night, he snuck into my tent and stole my phone! I woke up and realized

what had happened as he was leaving, then immediately got dressed and started chasing him."

"Safiq must have taken out the M E M O R Y C A R D and dropped the phone in the forest to get rid of the video evidence!" Pam guessed.

"Yep . . . at the same time as I was getting lost," Ramlee said bitterly.

"We can't let him get away with it," said Latifah fiercely. "We have to find out what he's hiding . . . **and we have to stop him**!"

Let's see . . .

Ramlee sighed. "How?" he asked. "We don't even know where Safiq is headed!"

"Maybe we don't . . .

but **IT'S NOT OVER YET**," Paulina said. Without another squeak, she scurried to her backpack and took out her camera.

LET'S REVIEW THE FACTS!

1) SAFIQ OFTEN MOVED AWAY FROM THE GROUP TO ANSWER MYSTERIMOUSE PHONE CALLS.

2) SAFIQ DISAPPEARED WITH ALL HIS STUFF, ABANDONING THE CAMPSITE.

3) RAMLEE'S PHONE WAS STOLEN BY SAFIQ, WHO PULLED OUT THE MEMORY CARD TO GET RID OF THE RECORDED VIDEO.

4) SAFIQ MAY BE IN CONTACT WITH TIMBER SMUGGLERS!

FiNALLY, THE TRUTH!

When Paulina's friends saw her camera, they immediately GUeSSeD what she had in mind. Ramlee wasn't the only one who'd been using a 🅒🅐🅜🅔🅡🅐 on the trip. Maybe Paulina had found a 🄲🄻🅄🄴 that would help track Safiq down!

"Let's see . . . the photos probably won't be very useful," said Paulina, scrolling to her videos.

Seated on the steps of the cabin, the Thea Sisters and their friends watched and **listened** carefully to every second of video. Paulina hadn't had any reason to film Safiq, but the guide might have come into the picture without realizing it.

"Hmm . . . I'm beginning to lose hope," Ramlee said at the end of the video filmed on the bridge. "What are the odds you

This will be tricky . . .

It's worth a try!

Let's see . . .

recorded a phone call between Safiq and his **partner**?"

"Very low," admitted Colette. "But very low is better than NONE!"

"You said it, sister!" Pam smiled. "Go on, Paulina. Show us the next one!"

The following video was SHOT at Lubuk Simpon, the natural pool. They saw themselves swimming, splashing in the water, and laughing happily. Then the picture moved to the shore. It stayed there, motionless, with the forest in the background.

"**What happened there?**" asked Violet. She leaned toward the screen to take a closer look.

Paulina thought for a second. "I remember now! I'd been taping you from the shore, and then you called me to **join** you swimming . . ."

"And you put down the camera and forgot to press the **STOP** button," Nicky added. "So it kept recording!"

The mice focused on the screen again — and saw someone new appear in the FRAME.

"It's Safiq!" Latifah squeaked. "Look! He's calling someone!"

Paulina tinkered with her camera to turn up the volume as high as it would go.

Safiq had been certain that the mice having fun in the water weren't listening to his conversation — but he didn't notice the camera *recording* everything he said a few feet away from him. He'd called his partner, and their conversation not only confirmed Ramlee's suspicions but also gave the mouselets more important new information.

By the end of the video, Latifah, Ramlee, and the **THEA SISTERS** were as sure as cheese on crackers.

"Now we know that Safiq is involved with **TIMBER** smugglers — and that he has an appointment with one of them right here in Taman Negara National Park!" Colette declared.

"Ramlee was right," Paulina added. "Safiq agreed to **accompany** our group only because he needed a cover for the meeting. And the meeting is tonight, at sundown, in the Kepayang Besar **CAVE**! The smugglers will probably give Safiq his share of the payoff. If only we could get a call out to the police!"

"We'll have to do **something**! We can't just let them get away with it," Nicky said.

"If we leave **RiGHt awaY**, we can get to the caves before sunset," Paulina suggested, pointing to the route on the map. "We can catch them in the act!"

"**I'M IN!**" agreed Colette.

"**Me too!**" said Ramlee.

"And me!" echoed Latifah.

"**Us too!**" Nicky said after exchanging a

look of agreement with Violet and Pam.

"So, what are we waiting for?" Pam sprang to her feet, smiling. "We have a lot of land to cover. Let's shake a tail. Kepayang Besar cave, **HERE WE COME**!"

MEETING AT SUNSET!

There was not a moment to lose. The group set out right away so they could try to reach Safiq's meeting spot before he and the smuggler got there. The mice **crossed** the jungle that separated them from the Kepayang Besar cave. They didn't get down in the snout — not even when it began to **drizzle**!

They had one very important mission: to find Safiq and the **smugglers** he was doing shady business with.

"Here we are," Ramlee announced when the group reached a **rock** wall. "They chose a very well-hidden place to meet! *Follow me!*"

Then he disappeared over a **GIANT** rock, which, the Thea Sisters discovered,

almost completely covered the entrance to the cave. At first, the mice used their flashlights to **SEE** until they found themselves in a large cave filled with natural light that came through an opening above.

"It's almost sunset," Nicky said. "We'd better hide."

"Yes, and remember to be very quiet," Latifah warned. "Our squeaks will echo around here."

The Thea Sisters, Latifah, and Ramlee **nestled** among the rocks piled up near the entrance. From there, the mice could **SEE** what was happening in the cave without fear of being discovered.

Shortly after they took cover, they heard someone approaching. Soon Safiq appeared!

"Anybody there?" the guide called out, looking around warily.

There was no answer. He took off his backpack and sat to **wait**. Meanwhile, safe in their hiding place, the Thea Sisters, Latifah, and Ramlee **watched** the scene in silence. They were careful not to make any noise or movement that would blow their cover.

The **mysterimouse** timber smuggler arrived a few minutes later. As he began squeaking with Safiq, the mouselets learned that their suspicions were correct: Safiq was not a smuggler himself, but he helped the **CRIMINALS** transport timber taken illegally from a rainforest through Malaysia and on to the rest of the world.

"You did well," the smuggler said, patting Safiq on the shoulder. "**You've earned your share!**"

When the smuggler pulled a yellow envelope from his pocket, the Thea Sisters had proof that Safiq was being paid for his role in the timber smuggling!

IT WAS TIME FOR ACTION!

Without a sound, the mice scurried out of their hiding places. They formed a **SEMICIRCLE** around Safiq and his accomplice.

"What are you doing here?!" Safiq cried.

"We've caught you red-pawed!" Nicky replied. "We came to stop you from ruining this **wonderful** place with your dirty business. I can't believe you could spend time in this beautiful place and still help to ruin it!"

The TIMBER smuggler frowned, irritated by the unexpected surprise.

"Safiq, do you know these little mouselings? How did they find us?"

"Don't worry! They're the group I used to get into the **park** without raising any suspicions," Safiq explained, acting tough. **Pointing** to Ramlee, he said, "At one point, he started playing detective.

But rest assured, I **destroyed** every bit of that evidence! They can't stop us."

The smuggler looked calmly at the mice around him.

"You'd better get out of here quickly! And don't get any funny ideas. No one is going to believe your BABBLE!"

"You may be right. Maybe no one will believe the babble of seven 'little mouselings,'" Paulina said with a sly smile. Then, pulling her camera out of her pocket, she declared, "But I think somebody is going to be very interested in this . . ."

She pressed **play**, and the phone call Safiq made to the smuggler at Lubuk Simpon rang out in the cave. Watching the video, Safiq turned as pale as BRIE.

"Give me that thing!" he growled, stepping toward Paulina.

"Go ahead," said Colette. "It's no problem! We've already **sent** this video to the police and to our journalist friends! They're already on their way here."

Suddenly, Safiq and the smuggler lost all the **CONFIDENCE** they had shown earlier. The two slowly backed toward the exit, then turned tail and scurried out of the cave, **disappearing** into the jungle.

"Great job!" Latifah squeaked.

"Hey, I'm curious," said Ramlee to Paulina and Colette. "How were you able to send the F O O T A G E from your camera? Does it have wireless internet?"

Colette winked. "We didn't! The two of them were too nervous to realize it was *IMPOSSIBLE*!"

"But as soon as we have an Internet connection, you can be sure we'll send it,"

Paulina told him. "Safiq and his accomplice are done with their illegal business!"

"Good for you, mouselets!" Ramlee said. **"You did it!"**

THE LAST
SURPRISE!

If that day was memorable, the **NIGHT** that followed was no different. After Safiq and the smuggler ran away, the Thea Sisters, Latifah, and Ramlee realized that it was **too late** to make the return trip to their tents. So while the **SUN** above the rainforest was giving way to the moon, the seven friends decided to spend the night right there, inside the Kepayang Besar **CAVE**. The mice fell asleep in the company of the bats that lived in the cave.

At the first light of **Dawn**, the friends headed back to their campsite.

"Great Gouda! I'm so glad to see you again!" Didier cried, *RUNNING* toward

them as soon as he saw them coming. "Ramlee! Are you okay?"

"Yes, everything is fine now!" Ramlee smiled gratefully. "Thank you so much for staying here and taking care of the camp and our equipment!"

"I was HAPPY to help," Didier said. "Listen, I have —"

Pam interrupted him as she hurried to rekindle the fire. "How about we have one last meal here before we go back?" she suggested.

Everyone was excited about that idea. After so much adventure, they were all happy to sit down and eat together! When they finished lunch, Didier cleared his throat and tried again to squeak what he had in mind.

"Mouse friends, I —"

But he was again interrupted. Paulina had stood up at the same time, and clapped her paws **LOUDLY**. "I think it's time for us to take down our tents and go home!" she said.

Didier planted himself in front of everyone, spread his arms wide, and **FINALLY** managed to make himself heard.

"Wait! Before we go, there's something I want to show you. **ANYONE INTERESTED?**"

"Sure!" said Violet, a little puzzled. **"Where are we going?"**

"It's a surprise," Didier said, winking at Latifah. "And this time, you can trust me! **I KNOW THE WAY!**"

Interested, the Thea Sisters, Latifah, and Ramlee followed Didier along a narrow path.

After a few minutes, they reached a small grassy clearing. At its center was the most **ENORMOUSE** flower the Thea Sisters had ever seen.

"Th-th-that's a . . ." Latifah stammered.

"A rafflesia!" Didier announced proudly.

He told them that in the previous days, while he'd been alone at the campsite, he'd started exploring around the area in search of the rare flower.

"I've made a mess of a lot of things, but in the end, I managed to **FIND** a rafflesia for you," Didier said to Latifah.

Gathered around that natural wonder, the Thea Sisters and their friends took a group PHOTO to remember their extraordinary adventure. It had been an unforgettable trip full of new discoveries, excitement, and heart-pounding action . . .

AND, MOST OF ALL, FRIENDSHIP!